D0011236

WELCOME TO
PASSPORT TO READING
A beginning reader's ticket to a brand-new world!

Every book in this program is designed to build read-along and read-alone skills, level by level, through engaging and enriching stories. As the reader turns each page, he or she will become more confident with new vocabulary, sight words, and comprehension.

These PASSPORT TO READING levels will help you choose the perfect book for every reader.

READING TOGETHER
Read short words in simple sentence structures together to begin a reader's journey.

READING OUT LOUD
Encourage developing readers to sound out words in more complex stories with simple vocabulary.

READING INDEPENDENTLY
Newly independent readers gain confidence reading more complex sentences with higher word counts.

READY TO READ MORE
Readers prepare for chapter books with fewer illustrations and longer paragraphs.

This book features sight words from the educator-supported Dolch Sight Words List. This encourages the reader to recognize commonly used vocabulary words, increasing reading speed and fluency.

For more information, please visit passporttoreadingbooks.com.

Enjoy the journey!

Little, Brown and Company
Hachette Book Group
1290 Avenue of the Americas, New York, NY 10104
Visit us at lb-kids.com

First Edition: April 2017

Little, Brown and Company is a division of Hachette Book Group, Inc.
The Little, Brown name and logo are trademarks of Hachette Book Group, Inc.

The publisher is not responsible for websites (or their content)
that are not owned by the publisher.

Library of Congress Control Number 2016949144

ISBNs: 978-0-316-26090-9 (pbk.); 978-0-316-55364-3 (ebook);
978-0-316-55365-0 (ebook); 978-0-316-43157-6 (ebook)

Printed in the United States of America

CW

10 9 8 7 6 5 4 3 2 1

Passport to Reading titles are leveled by independent reviewers applying the standards
developed by Irene Fountas and Gay Su Pinnell in *Matching Books to Readers:
Using Leveled Books in Guided Reading*, Heinemann, 1999.

THIRSTY DAY
IN THE
CRATER

Adapted by
Emily Sollinger

LITTLE, BROWN AND COMPANY
New York   Boston

DreamWorks

DINOTRUX

Attention, DINOTRUX fans!
Look for these words
when you read this book.
Can you spot them all?

Skya

Revvit

lake

rocks

It was a hot day.

The Dinotrux were

looking for water to drink.

"We have to get water fast!" said Ty.

"It is too hot to go fast," said Skya.

"I know of a stream," said Skya.
"Follow me!"

When they got to the stream,
there was no water.

D-Structs and Skrap-It

were also looking for water.

"We should follow Ty and
his Trux," said D-Structs.
"They will lead us to water.
Then we can take it for ourselves!"

Ty noticed that the Tortools
were wet.

"Look!" said Ty.

"The Tortools have been in water!"

"Tortools can swim," said Revvit.
"They know where to find water."
"We should follow them!" said Ty.

HISS! GROWL!

Did you hear that?" asked Ton-Ton.

It was D-Structs and Skrap-It.

"Protect the Tortools!" said Ty.

D-Structs and Skrap-It
tried to grab the Tortools.
"Leave them alone!" said Dozer.
"Get out of here, D-Structs," said Ty.

Skrap-It tried to tackle Ton-Ton.
"Bad move, dude," said Ton-Ton.

Skya tossed out a cord.

She grabbed the Tortools.

That was close," said Dozer.

"I am glad everyone is safe."

The Tortools went over a hill.

The Dinotrux followed them.

They found a lake.

"Water!" said Ty.

"You did it!" Dozer said to the Tortools.

"You found the water!"

Everyone took a big gulp of water.

"AHH!" said the Dinotrux.

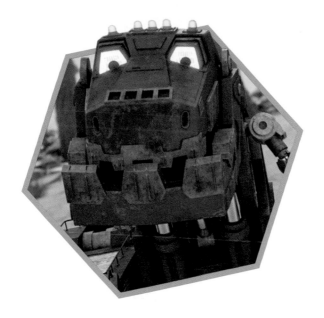

"I wish we could bring the lake
home with us," said Ty.
"We can build a river," said Revvit.
"Let's trux it up!" said Ty.

The Dinotrux moved rocks.

They cut wood.

They drilled holes.

They built a dam.

"Time to let the water flow!" said Ty.

"Wait!" said Skya.
Dozer was stuck
in the middle of the river.

The Dinotrux tried to plug the leaks.

The water rumbled.

The water splashed.

Dozer was still in the way.
The water was coming closer.

"These rocks are going
to break!" said Revvit.
"We cannot hold it
any longer!"

"You will not save him in time!"
said D-Structs.

The water rushed down.

The Tortools rolled toward Dozer.
They squeezed under his feet.
They rolled him away
from the water.

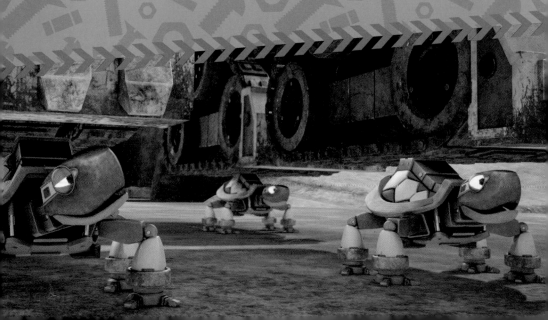

"All of this work has
made me thirsty!" said Ty.
"I will race you to
the water tank!" said Revvit.

The Dinotrux took turns
drinking water from the tank.

The Tortools splashed in the water.
A perfect end to a thirsty day
in the Crater.